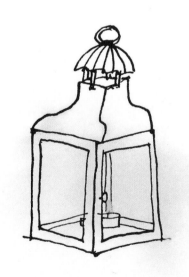

Translated by Ineke Lenting

Copyright © 2015 by Lemniscaat, Rotterdam, The Netherlands
First published in The Netherlands under the title *Kom je dansen, boze heks?*
Text copyright © 2004 by the heirs of Hanna Kraan
Illustration copyright © 2015 by Annemarie van Haeringen
English translation copyright © 2015 by Lemniscaat USA LLC • New York

First published in the United States and Canada in 2016 by
Lemniscaat USA LLC • New York
Distributed in the United States by Ingram Publisher Services

First U.S. edition 2016

Library of Congress Cataloging-in-Publication Data
Kraan, Hanna
Come and Dance, Wicked Witch / Hanna Kraan; illustrated by Annemarie
van Haeringen; translated by Ineke Lenting
p.; color illustrations; cm.

ISBN 978-1-935954-50-7 (hardcover)

1. Witches — Juvenile fiction. 2. Friendship — Juvenile fiction.
3. Animals — Juvenile fiction.

PZ7 [E]

Printing and binding: Worzalla, Stevens Point, WI USA

Come and Dance, Wicked Witch

Hanna Kraan &
Annemarie van Haeringen

Lemniscaat

The hare stood in the clearing in the middle of the forest. He drew lines in the sand with a stick.

The owl and the hedgehog ran up.

"Here we are!" the owl said.

"Why did you want us to come?" the hedgehog asked.

"I want to discuss something with you," the hare said. "What do you think about a big party, right here in the clearing?"

"Yes!" the hedgehog shouted, dancing around.

The owl also liked the idea. "Very nice," he said.

"When?" the hedgehog asked. "Tonight?"

"That's too soon," the hare said.

"Tomorrow night?" pleaded the hedgehog.

The hare thought for a moment and replied, "Let's do it the next day."

The hare pointed with his stick at the lines in the sand. "That's where the music is going to be. I want to ask the little rabbits to bring their horns and drums."

"Won't they be too loud?" the owl asked.

"No, it'll be fun!" the hedgehog said, adding "What's in that square?"

"That will be the snack table."

"The table should be bigger," the hedgehog said.

"It's going to be a gigantic table, because everbody will bring something to eat."

"I'll bake a bundt cake," the owl promised.

"Would you compose a party song as well?" the hare asked.

"Of course," the owl said, very pleased. He closed his eyes and mused, "Party time in the forest, party time in the woods…"

"Who's coming?" the hedgehog asked.

"It's going to be a party for everybody," the hare said. "Everybody is welcome."

The owl opened his eyes wide. "Even the wicked witch?"

"Of course. She lives in the forest too, doesn't she?"

"But what if she bewitches us?"

"She won't," the hare said, "not at a party. Come on, let's invite her now."

Swinging his stick, he went to the witch's cabin.

He knocked on the door. The door opened a crack and the witch peered out.

"What is it? I'm busy."

"There will be a big party the day after tomorrow in the clearing," the hare said. "Would you like to come?"

"No!" snapped the witch.

"Why not?"

"I don't feel like it and I don't have the time. I am preparing a very special potion that will keep me busy for days."

"But everybody will be there," the hare urged.

"And they all will bring something nice to eat," the hedgehog said. "What if you baked a cake…?"

"I won't be baking anything because I won't be coming," the witch snarled.

"It's going to be ever so nice," the hare said. "The little rabbits will make music."

"And I'll compose a party song," the owl said shyly.

"I am not coming," the witch said, slamming the door.

The hare sighed. "Pity," he said. "I was hoping that it would be a party for everybody."

"It's her choice," the owl said in a huff. "She won't hear my party song either."

The hedgehog kicked the door. "You're not invited anymore!" he shouted. "And if you do come, we'll chase you away!"

The hare pulled him away. "Leave her alone. Let's invite the others."

On the night of the party the witch was stirring her potion.

"Almost done," she muttered. "Add a bit of cobweb and then…"

Fragments of music came from outside.

"Oh, that'll be that party," the witch said. "Bunch of hooligans, yuck. Where was I? Oh yes. Cobweb and some pepper… stir it thoroughly… chopped nettles, tra-la-la, tweedle-dee-dee…" She hummed along with the music.

Suddenly she stopped stirring. She stared at the potion, wide-eyed. "What's happening?" she cried.

Poison-green foam bubbled up from the pot while smelly smoke filled the room.

Gasping, the witch opened the door.

She could hear the music very clearly now.

"It's gone wrong!" the witch moaned. "My potion is ruined after three days of work!"

She flung the wooden spoon onto the table and shook her fist at the door.

"It's because of all that noise outside! I can't even think. I'll make them pay!"

She took her broom and ran outside.

Loud singing rang out through the woods.

"Soon they'll sing a different tune," the witch said angrily. She jumped on her broom and flew to the clearing.

The animals didn't see her coming. They were all chatting and dancing.

The witch landed at the edge of the clearing and peeked at the party from behind a tree.

"First, I'll make those little rabbits disappear," she muttered. "That will give us some peace. Next, I'll make the table explode, and then I'll change the animals into toadstools. That'll teach them!"

She took a deep breath. "I'm HERE!" she yelled, marching into the clearing.

The little rabbits stopped tooting and drumming.

Everyone stopped dancing.

Suddenly all was quiet.

The hedgehog ducked behind the hare. "Chase her away!" he shouted.

The hare stood still for a second, totally surprised. Then, he walked up to the witch, his hand outstretched.

"How nice that you've come after all," he said warmly. "Take a seat."

"I won't sit down," the witch said icily. "I'm going to…"

The hare pushed her down on a chair.

"Here, have a piece of bundt cake," the owl said. "Homemade."

The witch tried to speak, but the hare didn't give her a chance.

"Now that it's quiet for a moment, we'll sing the owl's party song for you."

"No need,' the witch said, "because…"

"Our party song, just one more time! Special performance for the witch. One, two, three!"

"But…" the witch began.

Our woods are full of feasting
for young and for old
There's dancing and there's eating
come and join the fold

All the animals sang at the top of their voices.

The witch listened impatiently.
"Very nice. But *now*…"

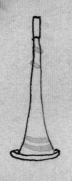

"*Now* we are going to dance," the hare said. He gave the little rabbits a wave and immediately the forest filled with music.

"All that noise…" the witch croaked. "That's why my potion…"

The hare took her hand and pulled her up.

"Come on, let's dance!" he called above the music as he whirled her about.

The witch looked around in despair. "How am I supposed to work my witchery?"

"You can do it!" the dancing hare called out. "Just copy me."

The witch stamped her feet in frustration.

"Great!" the hare shouted. "Now spin around."

Stiffly, the witch danced a few steps.

"I haven't come here to dance," she shrieked at the hare. "I have come here to bewitch you!"

"You may tell us all about it later. Now we're dancing."

The witch began to dance more wildly than ever.

"Bravo!" The animals cheered and danced all around her.

Finally the music stopped.

"Phew," the hare gasped. "I have to sit down for a minute. What did you say again? Something about witchery?"

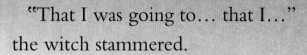

"That I was going to… that I…" the witch stammered.

"Yes?" the hare said.

The witch sighed. "That I was going to make you a witch's cake."

She snapped her fingers. Suddenly there was a party cake in the middle of the table, full of fruit and little flags.

"Hooray!" The animals cheered. "Long live the witch!"

The witch looked shyly at the ground.

The music rang out again.

The hedgehog pulled at the witch's sleeve.

"What do you want?" the witch asked. "Are you going to chase me away?"

"Of course not," the hedgehog said. "Would you like to dance?"

The witch danced with the
hedgehog and all the animals joined
them.

"What a nice party," the owl
called out at the hare.

The hare gave a satisfied nod.
"*A party for everybody!*"